Owls have big eyes so they can see at night,

And sharks have razor sharp teeth so they can bite.

Snakes have slippery skin they can shed like rubber,

And whales keep warm in cold water by using their blubber.

Giraffes have stretchy necks so they can feed up high,

And eagles have giant wings that let them fly.

Kangaroos have pouches to carry their young,

And the garden frog traps food on his sticky tongue.

Surely then it's not much to ask, that this lonely Ant Eater can do his task.

He has ears and toes; he just needs a nose,

Or a beak or a hooter to end his woes.

Nothing fancy or painted gold, just something to blow when he gets a cold.

So every night when I sleep and dream,

I imagine I have a brand new sniffing machine.

But when I awake it's the same old scene,

There's an empty spot where my nose should have been.

Then tell me this, and tell me true,

If my job is catching ants what can I do?

My clumsy paws are not the trick,

As those slippery ants are far too quick.

If I roar and bellow they simply scoff,

They point and laugh, and then run off.

They bury themselves in their anthill mound,

And blow me raspberries from underground.

I'm the laughing stock of all my peers,

The snoutless Ant Eater who no ant fears.

I cannot hunt and I cannot stalk,

What kind of Ant Eater eats his ants with a knife and fork?

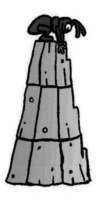

Something must be done, and done very fast,

If my reputation as an ant-catcher is meant to last.

Otherwise it's the same old strife,

For Arnold in his snoutless life.

Then one day there's a stroke of luck,

Rubbish falls from a garbage truck.

And stuck in the middle of all the muck,

Is a brand new hose from an Electrolux.

A little tape and some sticky glue,

And, Hey Presto! A nose like new.

A wonderful new stainless steel nose,

That swings from my ears and touches my toes.

A Wonderful, new pest-catching device,

Perfect for sniffing out ants and sucking up lice!

So now that I am fit and well,

I can sniff and snort and cough and smell.

Then those pesky ants will soon discover,

That they need to hide and run for cover.

Because Big Arnold is back and as proud as can be,

AND from this day on its ants for breakfast, dinner and TEA!!